Belle

By Andrea Posner-Sanchez

Illustrated by Atelier Philippe Harchy

Random House 🏠 New York

Copyright © 2005 Disney Enterprises, Inc. All rights reserved under International and Pan-American Copyright Conventions. Published in the United States by Random House Children's Books, a division of Random House, Inc., New York, NY 10019, and simultaneously in Canada by Random House of Canada Limited, Toronto, in conjunction with Disney Enterprises, Inc. RANDOM HOUSE and colophon are registered trademarks of Random House, Inc.

Library of Congress Control Number: 2004093750   ISBN: 0-7364-2327-3

www.randomhouse.com/kids/disney

MANUFACTURED IN CHINA

10 9 8 7 6 5 4 3 2

Can you keep a secret? Everyone knows I love to read. But I bet you didn't know that I also love to *write*.

The whole time I was held prisoner in the Beast's castle, I kept a journal. It's a secret journal that no one else has ever seen—not even my husband, the Prince!

I had come to the castle to rescue my father.
I promised the Beast I would stay in the castle
forever if he would just let my father go.

"Take me instead," I said.

I acted brave, but I was really scared.
Writing in a journal helped me feel better.

The Beast gave me my own room and said I could go anywhere in the castle, "except the West Wing!"

I wrote about the mysterious West Wing in my journal: *What goes on there?*

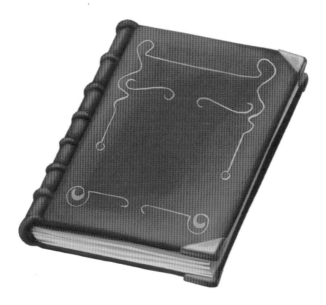

Every day I discovered more and more to write about. I had never seen such amazing things. The furniture spoke! The silverware danced! If I hadn't seen it with my own two eyes, I never would have believed it.

But keeping my journal a secret was
hard to do, since just about everything in
the castle was alive!

Sometimes I sat in the library and hid the journal inside another book. That way my new friends, Mrs. Potts, Cogsworth, and Lumiere, would think I was just reading.

When I wasn't writing in my journal,
I kept it hidden. I had to pick the hiding
spots very carefully.

Once, when the journal was behind a
curtain, Featherduster almost swept it out
the window!

And I thought I had lost my journal for good when Lumiere nearly set it on fire!

Can you believe I'm friends with a teapot, a candelabrum, and a clock?

I wrote a lot about Mrs. Potts, Lumiere, and Cogsworth in my journal.

They were so kind to me and always did
their best to make me feel at home. But I was
starting to get the feeling that they wanted me
to like the Beast!

How could I ever like someone so mean?

Everything changed after I sneaked
into the West Wing. That night I wrote
about it in my journal.

I know I wasn't supposed to, but I went to the West Wing today. I saw a magical rose floating under a glass dome. It must be important—the Beast yelled at me when I tried to touch it. I ran out of the castle and didn't stop until I was surrounded by wolves. Even though the Beast was angry with me, he saved me. Maybe the Beast isn't so mean after all. I would like to get to know him better. . . .

Soon after that, Mrs. Potts, Cogsworth, and
Lumiere arranged a lovely dinner for the
Beast and me. I was excited about spending
an evening with him.

Before heading downstairs, I hid behind the curtains and wrote in my journal: *I have a feeling something special is going to happen.*

Dinner was wonderful!

When we had finished eating, the Beast took my hand and asked me to dance. I had so much fun! I couldn't wait to write about it. It was a night I never wanted to forget!

After that, the two of us did lots of fun things together—and every night I wrote about them in my journal.

We went for long walks through the woods, and we read books to each other. My favorite time was when we fed the birds together!

I'm falling in love with the Beast!

At first I was too scared to tell him my
feelings, so I wrote about them instead. I filled
pages and pages of my journal with love notes.

My journal was complete the day I told the
Beast I loved him. He magically turned back into
the handsome Prince he once had been—and he
said he loved me, too.

*My dreams have come true! I can't wait
to spend the rest of my life with my Prince.*

Even though I'm now married to the Prince,
I still want to keep the journal secret. Will you
please help me keep my secret? Thank you!